Will's
Boomerang

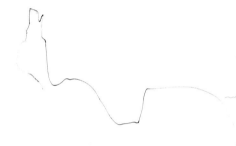

For my little cousin, Jacob with lots of love – SG

First published 2007
Evans Brothers Limited
2A Portman Mansions
Chiltern Street
London W1U 6NR

British Library Cataloguing in Publication Data

Gurney, Stella, 1975-
     Will's boomerang. - (Twisters)
     1. Boomerangs - Pictorial works - Juvenile fiction
     2. Children's stories - Pictorial works
     I. Title
     823.9'2[J]

ISBN-10: 0 237 53336 7 (pb)
ISBN-13: 978 0 237 53336 6 (pb)

ISBN-10: 0 237 53340 5 (hb)
ISBN-13: 978 0 237 53340 3 (hb)

Printed in China

Series Editor: Nick Turpin
Design: Robert Walster
Production: Jenny Mulvanny

TWISTERS

Will's Boomerang

Stella Gurney
and Stefania Colnaghi

Evans

This is Will.

Nice boomerang!

Boomerangs come back when you throw them.

7

Usually.

9

Better go and find it.

Mind the kangaroos!

Phew!

15

Keep searching, Will.

Look out!

That's right, Will – crocodiles!

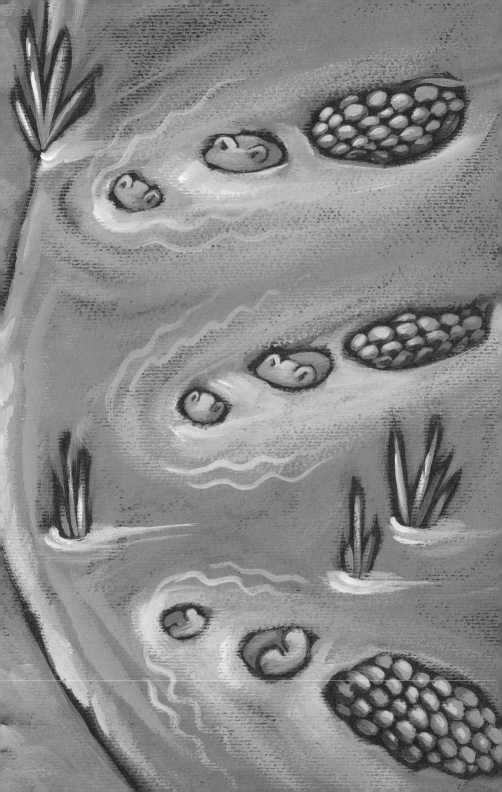

Time to go!

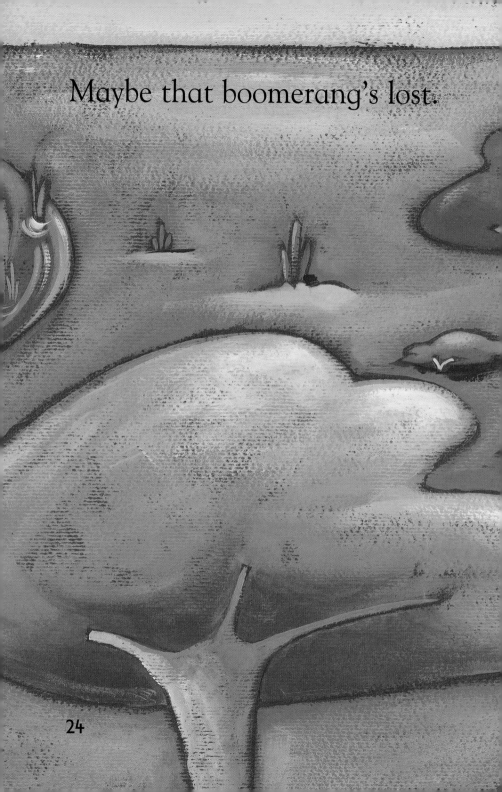

Maybe that boomerang's lost.

A snake!

27

Will's in trouble now.

Hooray! Will's boomerang came back!

Why not try reading another Twisters book?

Not-so-silly Sausage by Stella Gurney and Liz Million
978 0237 52875 1

Nick's Birthday by Jane Oliver and Silvia Raga
978 0237 52896 6

Out Went Sam by Nick Turpin and Barbara Nascimbeni
978 0237 52894 2

Yummy Scrummy by Paul Harrison and Belinda Worsley
978 0237 52876 8

Squelch! by Kay Woodward and Stefania Colnaghi
978 0237 52895 9

Sally Sails the Seas by Stella Gurney and Belinda Worsely
978 0237 52893 5

Billy on the Ball by Paul Harrison and Silvia Raga
978 0237 52926 0

Countdown by Kay Woodward and Ofra Amit
978 0237 52927 7

One Wet Welly by Gill Matthews and Belinda Worsley
978 0237 52928 4

Sand Dragon by Su Swallow and Silvia Raga
978 0237 52929 1

Cave-baby and the Mammoth by Vivian French and Lisa Williams
978 0237 52931 4

Albert Liked Ladders by Su Swallow and Tim Archbold
978 0237 52930 7

Molly is New by Nick Turpin and Silvia Raga
978 0237 53067 9

A Head Full of Stories by Su Swallow and Tim Archbold
978 0237 53069 3

Elephant Rides Again by Paul Harrison and Liz Million
978 0237 53073 0

Bird Watch by Su Swallow and Simona Dimitri
978 0237 53071 6

Pip Likes Snow by Lynne Rickards and Belinda Worsely
978 0237 53075 4

How to Build a House by Nick Turpin and Barbara Nascimbeni
978 0237 53065 5

Hattie the Dancing Hippo by Jillian Powell and Emma Dodson
978 0237 53335 9

Mary Had a Dinosaur by Eileen Browne and Ruth Rivers
978 0237 53337 3

When I Was a Baby by Madeline Goodey and Amy Brown
978 0237 53334 2

Will's Boomerang by Stella Gurney and Stefania Colnaghi
978 0237 53336 6